Moving Day

by Fran Manushkin

illustrated by Tammie Lyon

PICTURE WINDOW BOOKS
a capstone imprint

Katie Woo is published by Picture Window Books,
A Capstone Imprint
151 Good Counsel Drive, P.O. Box 669
Mankato, Minnesota, MN 56002
www.capstonepub.com

Printed in the United States of America in Stevens Point, Wisconsin.
102010
005990R

Library of Congress Cataloging-in-Publication Data
Manushkin, Fran.
    Moving day / by Fran Manushkin; illustrated by Tammie Lyon.
    p. cm. — (Katie Woo)
    ISBN 978-1-4048-5733-9 (library binding)
    ISBN 978-1-4048-6059-9 (paperback)
    [1. Moving, Household—Fiction. 2. Family life—Fiction.] I. Lyon, Tammie, ill. II. Title.
PZ7.M3195Mpd 2010   2009030618
[E]—dc22

Summary: When Katie Woo's family moves, she is sad about leaving her room to a stranger, and even more concerned that the new house will never feel like home.

Art Director: Kay Fraser
Graphic Designer: Emily Harris
Production Specialist: Michelle Biedscheid

Photo Credits
Fran Manushkin, pg. 26
Tammie Lyon, pg. 26

Table of Contents

Chapter 1
Dear New Girl

Katie's family was moving.

"You will love our new

house," said Katie's mom.

"I like this one!" said Katie.

"Why can't we stay here?"

"Your mom has a great
new job," said Katie's dad.
"We want to live close to it."

"Who will get my old
bedroom?" Katie asked.

"Another girl like you,"
said Katie's mom.

"I will write her a note," Katie decided.

"Dear new person," she wrote. "I hope you like this room. I loved it so much! Sincerely, Katie Woo."

Chapter 2

A Weird House

The Woo family drove away.

Katie's dad said, "Our new bathroom is great. It has a whirlpool bath."

"A whirlpool?" thought

Katie. "What if I spin around

and around and never stop?"

"Our new house has a sunken living room," said Katie's mom.

"Uh-oh," thought Katie, "what if I sink down into the floor and disappear? This house sounds weird!"

Suddenly, there it was!

The new house!

"It doesn't look spooky,"

thought Katie. "But you

never know."

Katie peeked into the

living room. "It's not sunken!"

she said.

"No way!" Her dad smiled.

"It's called 'sunken' because

it's a few steps down."

"Very fancy!" said Katie.

In the bathroom, Katie asked, "Where's the scary whirlpool?"

"It's not scary," said her mom. She turned on the whirlpool.

"Wow!" Katie said. "It's great for bubble baths!"

Suddenly, they heard a
loud wailing. It was coming
from the attic.

"Oh no!" Katie yelled.

"This house is haunted!"

Then a girl came running
into the house. She raced
upstairs.

Seconds later,
she came down,
holding a puppy.

"My puppy escaped from his travel box and hid in the attic. We almost left without him!" the girl said.

"I'm so glad you didn't," said Katie.

Chapter 3

Feels Like Home

Katie went to her bedroom to unpack.

Outside her window, she saw birds building a nest. "You are my new neighbors," Katie said with a smile.

Soon, Katie smelled

something wonderful.

"Mom is making wonton

soup!" she said.

Katie heard

pretty music too.

"And Dad is

playing the piano." Katie

smiled. "This place is starting

to feel like home."

As the family ate supper, Katie wondered, "Where's my bed?"

"I don't know," said her mom. "The store said it's coming today."

"I can sleep in the
whirlpool bath," Katie
teased. "It might be cozy,
but my blanket will get very
wet."

Just then, the doorbell rang, and in came Katie's bed.

"It's a bunk bed!" she yelled. "I can have sleepovers with Pedro and JoJo."

At bedtime, the moon
shone into Katie's room. It
lit up a piece of paper in
the corner.

It was a note! Katie read it.

"Dear new girl, I hope
you like this room. I did!
A lot!"

"I love it!" Katie decided.

"Good night, new room!"
she chanted, and she fell
asleep.

About the Author

Fran Manushkin is the author of many popular picture books, including *How Mama Brought the Spring; Baby, Come Out!; Latkes and Applesauce: A Hanukkah Story;* and *The Tushy Book*. There is a real Katie Woo — she's Fran's great-niece — but she never gets in half the trouble of the Katie Woo in the books. Fran writes on her beloved Mac computer in New York City, without the help of her two naughty cats, Cookie and Goldy.

About the Illustrator

Tammie Lyon began her love for drawing at a young age while sitting at the kitchen table with her dad. She continued her love of art and eventually attended the Columbus College of Art and Design, where she earned a bachelors degree in fine art. After a brief career as a professional ballet dancer, she decided to devote herself full time to illustration. Today she lives with her husband, Lee, in Cincinnati, Ohio. Her dogs, Gus and Dudley, keep her company as she works in her studio.

Glossary

disappear (diss-uh-PIHR)—to go out of sight

fancy (FAN-see)—very special or decorated

sincerely (sin-SIHR-lee)—in an honest and truthful way

sunken (SUN-kuhn)—below other areas nearby

wailing (WALE-ing)—letting out a long, loud cry of sadness or pain

whirlpool (WURL-pool)—a current of water that moves in a circle and pulls floating objects toward its center

Discussion Questions

1. At first, Katie was unsure about moving. Why do you think she felt that way?

2. Katie's new house felt more like home after she smelled her mom's soup and heard her dad playing piano. What sights, sounds, or smells remind you of your home?

3. Do you think it would be fun to move? Why or why not?

Writing Prompts

1. Pretend you are moving. Write a letter to the person who will move into your room.

2. Katie's new house has some special things, like a whirlpool tub and a sunken living room. Write a sentence about something special in your home.

3. Make a list of ten words that describe your home.

Having **Fun**
with **Katie Woo**

In *Moving Day*, Katie watches a bird build a nest outside her window. You can make your own nest with this fun project.

What you need:

- a brown paper lunch bag

- craft glue

- dried leaves, grass, and flowers

- optional: a bird and eggs from a craft store

What you do:

1. Open up the paper bag. Pull the bottom of the bag up toward the top. As you do this, the sides will crumple. Work with your bag to make it into a bowl shape.

2. Apply some glue to the bag, then stick a leaf on it. Repeat until your bag is covered with leaves. You can also glue on flowers or other lightweight items to decorate your bag.

3. Fill the bag with dried grass. If you would like, add a bird and eggs. Now you have a nest that looks as great as the real thing! Set it on a shelf or table for a pretty decoration.